Backyard Circus

by Jill Bryant
art by Stephen MacEachern

annick press
toronto + new york + vancouver

©2006 Jill Bryant (text)
©2006 Stephen MacEachern (art)
Edited by Pam Robertson
Design: Sheryl Shapiro

Annick Press Ltd.
All rights reserved. No part of this work covered by the copyrights hereon may be reproduced or used in any form or by any means—graphic, electronic, or mechanical—without the prior written permission of the publisher.

We acknowledge the support of the Canada Council for the Arts, the Ontario Arts Council, and the Government of Canada through the Book Publishing Industry Development Program (BPIDP) for our publishing activities.

Cataloging in Publication

Bryant, Jill
    Backyard circus / by Jill Bryant ; illustrated by Stephen MacEachern.

ISBN-13: 978-1-55451-012-2 (bound)
ISBN-10: 1-55451-012-0 (bound)
ISBN-13: 978-1-55451-011-5 (pbk.)
ISBN-10: 1-55451-011-2 (pbk.)

    1. Circus—Juvenile literature.   I. MacEachern, Stephen   II. Title.

GV1817.B79 2006   j791.3   C2006-901258-X

Distributed in Canada by:	Published in the U.S.A. by:
Firefly Books Ltd.	Annick Press (U.S.) Ltd.
66 Leek Crescent	Distributed in the U.S.A. by:
Richmond Hill, ON	Firefly Books (U.S.) Inc.
L4B 1H1	P.O. Box 1338
	Ellicott Station
	Buffalo, NY 14205

Printed in China.

Visit us at: www.annickpress.com

The publisher, author, and illustrator specifically disclaim any responsibility for any liability, loss, or risk (personal, financial, or otherwise) which may be claimed or incurred as a consequence, directly or indirectly, of the use and/or application of any of the contents of this publication.

This book was inspired by the Water Street Rats' backyard circuses in the late 1970s, performed by Max, Andrew, Pam, Dana, Lori, Paul, Ian, and me.

For Zoë and Mari and the next generation of backyard circus performers.
—J.B.

To Ethan and Kylie, my little acrobats, magicians, animals...
—S.M.

Contents

Let's Have a Circus! 4

Planning 6
Location, Ringmaster, Stage Manager, Performers, Doing Double Duty

Materials 12
Props and Equipment, Costumes, Face Painting

Main Acts 16
Clowning Around, Juggling, Animal Acts

Acrobatics 24
Gymnastics, Obstacle Course, Stilt Walking, Tightrope

Novelty Acts 34
Magic Show, Mime, Strongman

Come One, Come All! 42
Posters, Invitations, Tickets, Thank-You List

Big Top Time! 44
Final Go-Through, Spiffing Up, Behind-the-Scenes Setup

Step Right Up! 45
Shout It Out!, Go With the Flow, In a Muddle? Pandemonium Fix-It

After the Show 46
Thank you! Thank you!, Scrub, Wipe, and Polish, What's Next?

Fun Resources for Further Exploration 47
Circus Schools 48
About the Author and Illustrator, Acknowledgments 48

Let's Have a Circus!

Imagine the fun of creating your very own backyard circus! Let's bring on the clowns with silly hats and big shoes and the skillful jugglers who toss beanbags high in the air. Conjure up some pretend tigers, balancing on roly-poly balls. How about adding a stilt walker and some acrobats? With a long skipping rope stretched out on the grass, you can make your audience believe you are really teetering high above the ground. Then, just when your audience of moms and dads, friends, and relatives are sure you are going to fall way, way down, shock them all by pulling out a teacup and having a quick sip before you resume your death-defying act.

Getting the Show on the Road!

In this book, you'll find lots of fun ideas for main acts and performances, plus tips on setting up, selling tickets, collecting props and costumes, painting faces, and performing. By the end, you and your friends will have all the tools you need to put on your very own backyard circus show.

But keep in mind that the sample acts included in the book are suggestions only. I repeat, suggestions only! After all, the very best acts are the ones you make up yourself. When an idea is your very own, it could even turn into your trademark act—an act that everyone identifies with you. You can have fun picking and choosing bits and pieces from this book for your own circus. But you'll have a blast finding your own ways to make a rollicking good show. It's your personal touches that will really make the circus come to life. So, grab your silly hats and your fancy-dress costumes and head out to the backyard big top.

"Ladies and Gentlemen, Boys and Girls, step right up. The circus has come to town, and it's in your very own backyard!"

Now, let's get to it!

joke
Q: Why do horses run in circles?
A: Because it's hard to run in squares.

Circus Lore
Philip Astley, the Father of the Modern Circus, was an amazing trick-rider and horse trainer. He could balance on a cantering horse with one of his feet between his horse's ears while circling a sword above his own head. His horse Billy could lift a kettle from a fire and set up a teapot and cups for tea!

What's in a Word?
The Latin word *circus* really just means "circle," and was first used by the ancient Romans (who were absolutely wild about entertainment) to describe their arenas. Events such as horse-drawn chariot races, daredevil bareback riding, dancing elephants, acrobatics, wrestling, and gladiator battles took place in outdoor arenas where thousands of people could sit and soak up the action. Over time, the Roman events became more and more exotic and outrageous. It's recorded that at least one elephant was seen walking the tightrope!

The Greatest Show on Earth
The most famous circus of all time, and the first big show of the modern circus era, was the Ringling Brothers Barnum & Bailey Circus. This circus was out-of-this-world HUGE! They needed a whopping 100 railroad cars to move their show—more than twice as many as their next biggest competitor.

Planning

So, you're bursting with ideas and creative energy. How do you put it all together? Well, my friend, you need to make plans. Grab a notebook and pen, and let's get started!

Location

You might have a location in mind for the circus: your friend's backyard, a neighbor's front porch, or even your own family room. Pick a first and second choice. Ask the grown-ups who live at the places you choose if it's okay to use their space. Take turns practicing at every participant's home. This way you won't give the same parent a headache day after day with all your noise and hoopla. Then, closer to the date, you'll want to practice in the actual location, to get used to performing in the real space.

Decide how long you'll rehearse for—say two weeks? Six weeks? Do I hear eight weeks?

Ringmaster

The next step is picking someone to be in charge. The Ringmaster is in charge of all the acts and has several responsibilities. It's a good idea for the Ringmaster to be comfortable with public speaking, because he or she will introduce each act. A loud, clear voice is best so that everyone can hear. The Ringmaster should also be on the lookout for problems and know what to do to keep the action safe and entertaining.

Using circus language, or lingo, really adds to the atmosphere. Many people will be familiar with these common phrases from the circus. Have fun sprinkling your announcements with:

* **Ladies and gentlemen, boys and girls!**
* **Children of all ages!**
* **Come one, come all!**
* **Welcome to the greatest show on earth!**
* **Hurry, hurry, hurry!**
* **Step right up!**
* **See the incredible, the amazing, the spectacular, the unbelievable ...**

Pssst!
A female Ringmaster is called a *Ringmistress*. Historically, most famous Ringmasters have been men, but if you want to give the role of Ringmistress a whirl, step right up!

Circus Lore
In the early days of the circus, when horses were the main attraction, the Ringmaster was called the *equestrian director*.

Ringmaster Attire
* top hat
* red or black suit jacket "with tails" (the kind that makes you look like a penguin!)
* bow tie
* mustache (not for a Ringmistress, of course!)
* whistle

Mind the Gap
Sometimes the circus stage will be empty, say when all the performers have to change costumes. When there is nothing happening and a "lag" results, the Ringmaster can keep the audience interested. The last thing you want to hear is Aunt Mildred asking, "Is it over yet?" Instead, keep the buzz of excitement in the air. The Ringmaster should have a quick trick or two to use during unexpected gaps in the show. Play a goofy tune on the harmonica or kazoo, recite a simple rhyme, demonstrate your skills with a yo-yo, or tell a bunch of corny jokes. Even the old trick of rubbing your tummy and patting your head will keep the audience entertained.

New Wave
The first modern troupe to change our idea of circuses was Australia's Circus Oz, founded in 1977 and still going strong. Circus Oz uses some traditional acts in its animal-free show, but it is mainly a mix of acrobatics, live rock music, and acts that poke fun at society. Audiences are wowed by fireballs, disco juggling, and human cannonballs. They even have a clown who walks upside down along the ceiling! (He actually wears specially designed magnetic shoes that fit into tracks!)

Stage Manager

Who is happiest holding a pencil, listing details, making plans, and getting stuff done? If you guessed the Stage Manager, you're right! The Stage Manager is the main organizer of all the things you'll need for your circus.
—Does that sound like you?
—Uh, huh.
—Was that a "yes"? Okay, then hop to it, partner! If your friend Ada has a princess costume that you're going to use, write that down on your list of materials. Then, before the show, you can remind Ada what to bring.

Tracking props and costumes is part of every Stage Manager's job in the world of theater and performance, circuses included. Without the Stage Manager's detailed lists and records, important props might be missing for the grand performance. So—drumbeat, please (*boom, ba ba boom, boom, ba ba boom*)—have no fear, get in gear, the Stage, Stage, Stage Manager's here—or something like that!

Performers

Start seeking performers by asking all of your friends and other kids who live in your neighborhood: "Hey, do you want to be part of the coolest, zaniest, craziest, scariest, wildest, simply excellent event-of-the-century backyard extravaganza?" When they say, "Wha-aa-at's that?" you tell 'em, "It's a backyard circus! Want to join?"

Write down the names of the kids who want to be in the circus—the "performers." You can create a wonderful neighborhood circus with 4 to 12 kids—but the more the merrier.

Scheduling

Scheduling rehearsals is another important part of the Stage Manager's job. During the planning and practicing stages, you might have to focus on just a few of the acts at a time if some friends are away on holidays.

Who's Got Talent? Everyone, Of Course!

Keep track of any special talents and skills the performers have. Can you tell funny jokes? Can your friend do a handstand? Does your cousin Samantha take ballet lessons? Can your neighbor Jack bounce on a pogo stick? Whatever skills you and your friends have, they can all be used in your circus.

The Birth of Cirque

Montreal-based Cirque du Soleil is one of the most popular circuses touring today. From day one, in 1984, it has featured non-traditional performances by street entertainers such as fire-eaters, magicians, and storytellers mixed with more usual circus artists including trapeze and tightrope artists. Their costumes, which are over-the-top outrageous, combine with fantastic lighting effects that help transport audiences to another world. One-of-a-kind musical scores link all the acts to the main story or theme. Like many other modern circuses, the acts are all animal-free.

Calling All Brains!

Pick a date for a rollicking brainstorming session. This is where you get down to the nitty-gritty planning. Talk about

* main acts
* short acts
* special talents
* fabulous costumes
* neat props

Brainstorming sessions tend to be very loud. Make sure everyone has a chance to be heard! Listen up, performers. One friend may have the idea of a lifetime, and you don't want to miss it. One idea can lead to another, which leads to another, and so on! Ask the Stage Manager to record all the ideas.

No-Nonsense Noodling

Circuses usually have a director, who tells the performers where to stand, when to turn, and how to speak, but for a neighborhood show the best way is to play. Play? That's right, play! By playing with the acts and doing them over and over, kids can shout out: "Hey, why don't we try this?!" See which suggestions work best. Some people call this process *noodling around*. When you practice by noodling around, you can all have a hand in directing.

Doing Double Duty

After you've settled on a Ringmaster, a Stage Manager, and your performers, you still have to double up and assign more jobs.
—More! How could we possibly have more jobs?
—Well, to make the circus complete, you'll need people to be in the support crew, too. I'm talking about the ticket takers, the ushers, and the decorators.

Ticket Taker

The ticket taker collects tickets from the guests as they arrive. The ticket taker should arrive half an hour *before* the show. Now be prepared. Not everyone will come with a ticket, so the ticket taker may have to sell some tickets and will need to have change available, plus know how to count! Make a good first impression with your guests by chatting or getting them in a circusy mood by telling jokes. Grab a megaphone and shout out that the circus is starting soon. Wear the costume you need for your first circus act while you're doing your double duty of collecting tickets.

Ticket Taker Equipment

* ticket booth or table
* stools or chairs (optional)
* tickets
* money box
* change (coins and a few bills)
* megaphone

—Okay, let me see if I have this straight. The ticket taker should be good at math, always be on time, and like chatting?
—You got it! Hey, are you volunteering?
—Uhhh ...
—Excellent! I'll take that as a "yes."

This Way, Madame

Volunteers can show guests to their seats just like ushers at a theater. Ushers make sure no one sits in the circus ring or performing area. They can hand out programs if you've made them.

Make-Your-Own Megaphone

The Ringmaster, ticket takers, and performers can make sure they come through loud and clear by using megaphones.

Materials
* large sheet of bristol board
* large circular object, such as a small garbage can lid or a huge pot lid
* small circular object, such as an unopened can of beans
* pencil, scissors, tape, stapler
* markers, stickers, glitter glue (optional)

1. Trace a humongous circle onto the bristol board and cut it out.
2. Fold the bristol board in half to make a crease.
3. Cut the bristol board along the crease to make two half-circles.
4. Fold the straight edge of one of the half-circles in half. Mark the center point on that edge with a dot.
5. Draw a straight line from the center point to the outside of the circle to form a pie-shaped wedge that is one-third of the size of this half-circle. Cut along the line and recycle the small wedge.
6. Take the larger section of the half-circle and use a small circular object to trace a smooth curve along the pointed end. (This will be the mouthpiece.) Cut along the curve.
7. Decorate one side of the paper with markers, stickers, and/or glitter.
8. Roll the paper into a cone shape with the straight sides together. Staple the wider end of the bristol board, then tape the edges at the mouthpiece.
9. Cut out a long, skinny rectangle of bristol board to make a handle.
10. Attach the handle to the megaphone with a staple and some tape. Make a second megaphone with the other half-circle.

Roustabouts

Besides being able to boast about having this cool-sounding job title, roustabouts are the behind-the-scenes strong folks who heave-ho all the heavy equipment and set pieces into place. They transform the backyard into a real live circus ring. They also take apart the circus equipment at the end of the show. In a backyard circus, everyone will be a roustabout. You'll need all hands on deck to set up and take down the stuff you need for your show. The Stage Manager can keep everybody organized and tell them (nicely!) what to do next.

Materials

Props and Equipment

You can add a lot of pizzazz to a show with some basic props and equipment. Props are items that performers use, such as balls, skipping ropes, and magic wands. Equipment includes things such as a tape player, chairs for the audience, and small tables. There could be a lot of stuff to find, but have no fear. It's easy. First of all, do you have a garage? Raid it. Is that a rope sticking out from under the rec-room couch? Snatch it. Check out second-hand stores and look through storage closets with your grandparents. When you find something really great, you might want to create a whole act around it just to be sure you can use it.

Okay, now "organization" is the name of the game here, so let's get to it. Grab a pen and your circus notebook. Create your own lists using the headings "Props" and "Equipment." The number of materials you'll need will depend on the acts you create.

Ideas for materials:

PROPS
ball
balloons
beach towels
bucket
handkerchief
hula hoops
juggling balls
magic wand
musical instruments
rubber snakes and bugs
skipping ropes
umbrella
whoopee cushion

EQUIPMENT
old mattress/blankets
inner tube
inflatable pool toys
magician kit
old sheets
puppets
stilts
stool
CD/tape player
CDs or tapes
tricycles and/or bicycles
wagon

Costumes

This is where the fashionista in you has a chance to get really creative. Be bold, be wild, be crazy. Discover the pizzazz that costume design can bring to the world of performing.

—Okay, picture this: You've got a too-small ruffled skirt and an old lampshade. These items might seem useless to the untrained costume expert, but in your hands they will be the basis for a fabulous clown costume.

—Really?

—Yup. Wear the ruffled skirt around your neck to form a ruffled clown collar. Then put the lampshade on your head. Goodbye lampshade, hello clown hat. Are you getting the hang of it now?

—Yeah, I think so. Would my dad's shoes look good with this costume?

—You betcha, my friend. You totally get it now. Experiment, invent, and create. There are sooooo many possibilities.

Some ideas for circus costumes
(see also the Main Acts and Novelty Acts sections)

animal costumes
clown costume
pirate costume
princess costume
superhero costume
apron
bathrobes
bodysuits
bow tie
cape
costume jewelry
fairy wings
fake eyeglasses
fake mustache or beard
oversized shoes or boots
pajamas
raincoat
rubber boots
scarves
silly hats
striped socks
sunglasses
ties
tights
top hat
tutus
vests
wigs

Face Painting

Face paint can transform you completely. Believe it or not, your own mother might not recognize you.

Rev Up the Wow Factor

Add a little face paint or makeup to your look. For best results, design your face on paper ahead of time. Color in the drawing with different shades of makeup. See if you like it on paper before painting your face for real, then practice painting your face in front of a mirror. You might want to ask a friend or a grown-up to help you apply the makeup.

Materials
- water-soluble makeup
- brushes and sponges
- small dish of water
- hair elastics or headband
- soap and water for washing

Water-soluble makeup comes shaped like round paint palettes or sticks that look like crayons. It is easy to put on and take off. You can wash it away with soap and water. If you buy the palette kind, you'll also need to use some cosmetic or soft art brushes.

To Paint or Not to Paint?

Do you have five different characters to play? If so, you'll probably want to skip the face painting. It's way too much work to wash off your makeup and repaint your face between each act. You'll be busy enough changing your costume and gathering your props. So, if you have multiple roles, it's time to put those face muscles to work!

Open your eyes up wide, raise your eyebrows, and open your mouth. That's "surprise."

Lower your eyebrows and clench your teeth tight. That's "anger."

Happy characters have big smiles and eyes that sparkle with laughter.

Experiment with different facial expressions to show every type of mood.

Some kids and grown-ups find white-faced clowns downright scary. You can create a softer, friendlier version by leaving your face unpainted and just adding a red nose, sparkles, and colorful circles on your cheeks. Combine this with a funny wig and a clown costume and you'll still look like a clown, but you won't scare anyone!

"O" Me, Oh My!
Cirque du Soleil is known for their fantastic costumes and frequent costume changes. In Cirque's Las Vegas show called "O," synchronized swimmers actually had to change their costumes underwater!

Thinking BIG
Gesturing with your whole body

* **pointing**
  Stretch your whole arm and point with one finger. Lean toward the pointing finger.
* **shrugging**
  Lift both shoulders, bend your arms, and stretch your hands out, palms up.
* **yawning**
  Place your hand over your mouth and lean over to one side.

Clown
Here's how to make a simple clown face.
1. Tie back hair.
2. Wet a small sponge with water.
3. Dab some white makeup onto the sponge.
4. Apply a white base to the face.
5. Use a brush to paint a red nose.
6. Outline a large red mouth with the same brush.
7. Clean your brush, or choose a new one.
8. Paint on high, arched eyebrows in another color.
9. Fill in the space under the eyebrows with a third color.
10. Add cheek circles in a fourth color.
11. Wash your brushes and sponges in soap and water.

Masquerade
Here's another idea: wear a mask. Masks are usually easy to get on and off, so they work great for kids with lots of parts to play. Now, here's the catch: masks don't change or move. Each mask can show only one expression. When you perform with a "frozen" face, it's important to make your gestures and movements extra BIG to bring your character to life.

joke
Q: Why did the elephant quit the circus?
A: Because she didn't want to work for peanuts!

Main Acts

Clowning Around

Nothing says "circus" better than a funny clown in an outrageous costume. With jokes and crazy stunts, clowns will keep your audience roaring with laughter.

Pick a Mood, Any Mood

Clowns often have exaggerated facial expressions. Happy clowns have a huge, smiley face painted on. Sad clowns have a mouth that turns down and a tear painted on their cheek. Your posture and gestures can signal a clown's mood, too. If you hang your head, you will look sad. If you chew your fingernails or wring your hands, you'll look nervous. If you kick up your heels and stretch out your arms, you'll look excited. Practice displaying different moods by rehearsing in front of a mirror. Choose the mood you like best and base your character on it.

To Talk or Not to Talk?

Some clowns like to tell jokes. Others are silent. Clowns who don't speak use mime, gestures, and stunts. With mime, you can make the audience believe pretty much anything. As you walk along the ground, mime that you are at the top of a tightrope wire, standing on a platform. Peer down and pretend to be scared of heights. *Eeeeeeee!* Make your body shake and quiver. To finish this stunt, pretend to jump down into a small pool of water. It might take you several attempts before you actually jump. The more false starts you have, the more the audience will laugh.

Laughs Between Acts

Clowns are very useful to have around. They can fill in the time between acts when the other performers need to change their costumes. Each time you, as a clown, appear between acts, you could do a similar stunt or joke. The first time, do silly, sloppy somersaults. The second time, jump rope, but get tangled up. The third time, do the "hula" with a hula hoop that always lands—*thunk!*—on the ground.

Pssst!

- **The classic clown** with white face paint is called a "white-faced clown." This clown is usually intelligent and neatly dressed, and may be the boss.
- **An "Auguste clown"** has a red nose, an oversized costume, and is clumsy.
- **A "character clown"** looks more ordinary and may be dressed to show a certain role or job. This clown could be anything from a hobo to a ballet dancer. Character clowns use black makeup to play up their eyes and eyebrows.

How to Dress

Find a pair of baggy pants, a tight jacket, and a goofy hat. Put them on and make a silly face. Do you look funny? A polka-dot bow tie, gigantic boots, and striped socks can help to pull together a clown costume. Just one glimpse at a clown's silly outfit can be enough to make the audience chuckle. These baggy clothes will probably feel different from your regular clothes, so wear your costume when you practice. This will help you develop your clown's character better, too.

Make a Clown Nose

Materials
* a cardboard egg carton
* scissors
* red paint
* a hole punch
* sewing elastic

1. Cut one egg cup from the center of the carton. Trim the corners.
2. Paint the egg cup red and let it dry.
3. Punch holes on two opposite sides of the egg cup. Thread a length of elastic through each hole and tie it.
4. Place the clown nose on your nose and tie the elastic behind your head.

Juggling

Send a shiver of tension through the audience by throwing objects into the air and making unbelievable catches! When something could go wrong at any second, jugglers know they've got the crowd right where they want them.

Juggling Balls

Juggling is a skill that takes a lot of practice. When you are trying to learn, it is best to use real juggling balls from a toy store or dollar store. The balls should all be the same size and weight. These balls won't hurt if you—*whoops!*—drop them on your toe. Juggling balls make a fantastic *fwack* sound when they hit the ground. The great thing about this is that the filling stops them from going *bo-o-oing* and bouncing away every time you drop one. If you have to keep stopping to search for a lost ball, you waste valuable juggling time.

Time Warp

Juggling goes way, way back in time. The first time juggling was performed was about 4,000 years ago in Egypt, where entertainers would juggle for royalty. Part of a large picture in an ancient tomb in Egypt shows three girls juggling with balls. They are joined by girls doing acrobatics: a back walkover, spins, and leaps.

Warm Up

Begin by tossing one ball into the air and catching it with the same hand. Get to know how the ball feels. Try to toss the ball with the same force each time. Throw the ball to eye level. When you're comfy doing this with one hand, toss and catch the ball with your other hand. This simple exercise gets you used to the weight of the balls and makes you more relaxed about tossing them with either hand.

—Hey! Are you still reading! Get up! Get those juggling balls and hop to it! That's the way.

Next, toss the ball in an arc with your left hand and catch it with your right. Then switch.

—Easy-peasy, right?

Now you're ready to toss two balls. With a ball in each hand, toss the balls straight up at the same time. Catch the balls in the same hands. Do this several times to get a feel for using two balls. You don't do this in real juggling, but it is a good practice exercise.

The Real Thing: 2 Balls

And now for the really fun stuff! Follow these steps to juggle (for real!) with two balls:

1. Place a small juggling ball in each hand.
2. Throw the ball in your right hand in an arc to your left hand.
3. When this first ball is at the highest point in the arc, quickly toss the second ball in an arc from the left to the right hand.
4. Catch the first ball in your left hand and the second ball in your right hand. Practice until the motion is smooth. See how many times you can toss the balls without dropping either one.

The Real Thing: 3 Balls

Once you have perfected two-ball juggling, you can introduce a third ball. Juggling with three or more objects is much trickier, but practice makes perfect.

1. Hold two balls in one hand (ball #1 and ball #3) and one ball in the other hand (ball #2). Practice two-ball juggling again (with ball #1 and ball #2), keeping ball #3 in the same hand as you juggle the other two.
2. After a lot more practice, and when you feel ready, toss ball #3 when ball #2 is at eye level. Don't worry too much about catching at this stage. Focus on making your three throws.
3. Once you master the throws, try to catch ball #1 and ball #3. It's okay if you drop #2 at this stage.
4. Keep practicing until you keep all three balls in constant motion.

Creative Juggling Props

Other small objects make good juggling props—just avoid juggling any objects that have sharp points or could break. Try oranges, balls of string, and glue sticks. Turn the juggling act into clowning by stopping to eat an orange, getting tangled up in string, or getting all sticky with glue.

Here's a list of other fun props to juggle:
* large plastic rings
* plastic bowling pins ("juggling clubs")
* beanbags
* small stuffed animals
* water balloons
* scarves

Juggling requires good *hand-eye coordination*. Hand-eye coordination occurs when we see something with our eyes and instantly react by moving our body in a certain way. For example, while juggling, when we see that a ball is at the top of its arc, we have to throw the next ball.

Circus Lore
When the legendary Ringling brothers were still children, a traveling circus came to their town. Their dad scored some free tickets and their lives were changed forever. Soon after, the brothers put on their own backyard circus, including some very daring juggling stunts. Using what he could find around the house, big brother Al even juggled his dad's hats and his mother's plates. *Yikes!*

Practice
Practice juggling by yourself every day. Find a quiet, uncluttered place where you can focus. Think about juggling. Nothing else. Juggling. Juggling. Juggling.

Now What?
How's it going? Are you a lean, mean juggling machine? If so, get performing! If not, don't despair. Keep trying. In the meantime, you can work your juggling attempts into a hilarious clown act that ends with balls all over the ground. This is the fun of creating your own circus!

Other Circus Tricks

There are lots of other cool circus gizmos that are fun to try. Many of these are related to juggling and can be found at toy and game stores.

Yo-Yo Tricks

When you start off with a new yo-yo, you need to measure the string and cut it to the right length for your height. Then make a slipknot at the end that your middle finger fits through. Wind the string around the axle. Hold the yo-yo in your hand, palm up, with the loop around your finger. Let 'er roll and see if you can make the yo-yo "sleep"— this is when it spins at the bottom. With practice, you can learn how to do other cool tricks.

Plate Spinning

Plastic, non-breakable spinning plates are fun to try out. It doesn't take too long to learn how to balance and spin a specially designed plate on the end of a stick. More advanced tricks, however, take time to master. You can make your own version of a spinning plate with a Frisbee and a wooden dowel. *Wheeeee!*

Devil Sticks

Devil stick sets are made up of two hand sticks and a slightly larger juggling stick. The hand sticks have a special gluey coating on them that helps the performer "grab" the juggling stick with the hand sticks. Using one or two hand sticks, the performer moves the whirling juggling stick in all kinds of incredible ways.

Diabolo

A diabolo is made up of two sticks joined by a string and a spool. The spool resembles two hollow domes that are joined to make an hourglass shape. Holding a stick in each hand, performers can launch the spool way up into the air and then catch it on the string again when it falls.

Animal Acts

Bring out the hoops and exercise balls. The animals are in the ring!

Looking Back

Animals were the stars of the first circuses in Rome. They were used again in the late 19th century, when the modern circus was born. Animals were main attractions until the 1980s. It's true that there are some circuses that still use animals today, but for the most part animal acts are a thing of the past. Circuses of long ago featured animals of all shapes and sizes. The more exotic the better. They even included hippopotamuses, zebras, gorillas, and camels.

Animal Rights

In the United States today, the Ringling Brothers and Barnum & Bailey Circus and the Big Apple Circus use animals in their performances. These circuses must care for the horses, dogs, and elephants very well. Today's circuses must obey strict laws that protect animals. These guys can't even think about including endangered critters like giant pandas.

Pssst!

A *menagerie* is a collection of wild animals, such as elephants, camels, and tigers. It can also refer to the backstage area where the animals are kept.

Performance Tip

You might want to plant a few of your performers in the audience to start clapping wildly when the dog does the sequence of tricks. This will encourage the whole audience to join in.

Dressing Up

How about dressing up as a lion, a tiger, a dog, a bear, an elephant, or a horse? Make a lion, dog, or bear costume by dressing in brown clothes and fastening paper ears onto a hair band. Create paws by wearing socks on your hands, paint your face, and you're all ready to roar! Try to move like the animal you're impersonating. Take big, heavy steps if you are a bear. Walk on all fours to be a dog or a lion.

It's easy to have a pretend animal perform all sorts of neat tricks. Choose a trainer and grab some props. Hoops, exercise balls, and low stools work wonderfully. For an act that packs a wallop, cover the space inside a hula hoop with one layer of tissue paper. Tape the tissue paper around the edges of the hoop. Now have your animal partner jump through the hoop. *Crash!* The light tissue paper will make a loud sound as the animal pounces through the hoop.

Of course, it might be funnier if the animal misbehaves on purpose and outsmarts the trainer. When asked to shake a paw, the kid dressed as a dog could roll over. When asked to roll over, the poorly trained dog could sit up. The trainer could become more and more frustrated, until finally the goofy dog does the entire sequence of tricks correctly, perhaps while the trainer's back is turned!

Performers dressed as animals can also jump ropes, ride bicycles, and play musical instruments.

Potty Jokes

If you have horses in your act, you'll have to clean up the poop! Have a clown rush out with a broom and dustpan. The clown can make a big show of sweeping the stinky mess into the dustpan while waving the air to keep the stink away from her nose.

Toy Animals

Stuffed animals may not be able to move on their own, but with a little help from the animal trainer—that's you—they can do spectacular soaring somersaults. Make your stuffed monkey soar high in the air. You can also leap onto a hobbyhorse and prance around the ring. Wave to the cheering audience and blow kisses to your fans.

Acrobatics

Gymnastics

Astonish the crowd with your flexibility as you roll, swing, jump, and *leee-eee-eap* across the circus ring! Whether you are dressed as a clown, an elegant gymnast, or a member of a tumbling team, your cool gymnastics stunts will captivate the crowd.

Tumbling

Tumbling is so much fun! Forward and backward rolls are basic tumbling moves. Cartwheels, walking on your hands, and front and back walkovers will add even more excitement (and soaring height) to a tumbling act.

There are many ways to perform a tumbling act. You could have a team of tumblers who perform the same moves in a line. Another way is to have a solo or duet performance with one or two circus performers. You could dress up as clowns and tumble across the ring. If you try a clown act, practice making tumbling moves that are funny, such as a clown trying over and over to do a front roll, and getting stuck in the middle every time.

Contortion

Imagine floor gymnastics and yoga. Then put them together. Twist and stretch your body into an unbelievable position. Now hold it. *Whew!* This is the art of contortion. Poses are positions you hold completely still, as if you're a statue. Balances are really hard poses that you try to hold perfectly still, often with a partner or two. You can't learn super-bendy moves overnight, but there are lots of simple poses and balances that are very doable and will impress the crowd.

Circus Alphabet

Here's a great way to limber up *and* put together a fun act. Bend your body to form all the letters of the alphabet—A, B, C, D, and so on. Team up with another performer to form letters such as W and X. Do you have enough kids to spell the word CIRCUS?

joke
Q: What season is it when you're on the trampoline?
A: Springtime!

Balancing
Combine gymnastics skills with balancing skills to produce mesmerizing results!

Acrobatics
Real live circus performers don't only do acrobatics on the trapeze; super-cool stunts take place right in the middle of the circus ring, on the ground. Working in pairs, circus performers can balance on top of one another and make neat shapes. It usually looks a bit tricky and, yup, the performers need excellent balance to make it work.

Pssst!
Circus performers are sometimes called *kinkers*, but that was originally the nickname for acrobats.

Pyramid
To make a human pyramid, you need six kids. Make sure the biggest kids are at the base of the pyramid, then climb aboard! You can also make a simple pyramid with just three kids.

Duet
Here is a fun duet balance that you can try with a friend.
1. Decide who is the stronger. That person will be the "base." The other acrobat will be the "top."
2. The base person lies on her back with legs bent and arms extended straight up toward the sky.
3. The top person cups her hands over the base person's knees. Next, the top person puts one knee, then the other, on top of the base person's hands.
4. The top person should point her toes and keep her head in line with her body. Try not to wiggle!

Tip:
Hey kids! Wear simple, stretchy clothes to do acrobatics. Leotards or bodysuits are great, but shorts and a T-shirt would be fine too. To show off your moves best, wear clothes that hug your body. Baggy shirts and long, loose pants will hide the neat shapes your body is making. Some acrobats might like running shoes, but bare feet work best.

Obstacle Course

Acrobats and clowns love to show off their super-fast speed and athletic talents with this tricky obstacle course. You can even let the audience join in the fun!

Materials
You can make a great obstacle course with materials from your home. Check out the garage, basement, or storage closet for items such as these:

- inner tubes
- hula hoops
- lawn chairs
- inflatable pool toys
- skipping ropes
- cardboard boxes
- large pail
- board
- towels
- ball
- garden hose
- beanbags

Hop, Climb, Jump, Swing
The origins of obstacle courses actually go back to military boot camps. At training camps, recruits undergo tough physical exercises. Grueling obstacle courses are set up to make people push themselves to their physical limits. The result is a bunch of confident recruits in tip-top shape.

Get Ready
Arrange the materials you have collected into a fun and safe course. You'll want to place the equipment for each station in a line or circle so that it is clear where to begin and end the course. Every obstacle course is different and will depend on the types of materials you have on hand. Set up a fun and wacky course that involves activities like climbing, jumping, turning, rolling, and throwing. You can also include circus tumbling moves and use homemade gymnastics equipment, such as a

simple balance beam laid on the ground.

Add bits and pieces of events from track and field as well. Hurdle over a skipping rope tied between lawn chairs. Set up a higher rope to make a high jump. Including posts like these in your obstacle course guarantees that you'll have some spectacular leaps for the audience to admire.

To add to the fun, you can also have stations on the course where participants need to gallop in a circle, jump through a hula hoop, or put on a silly hat before going on to the next point. You could also include a carnival event like a beanbag toss, where performers must throw a beanbag into a bucket while standing behind a line on the ground. Whatever you do, make sure it will be fun to watch. The obstacle course circus act should keep the crowd captivated by your tricky physical feats.

Get Set
Line up single file so you can complete the course one after another in a follow-the-leader style. Dress up like clowns, acrobats, or circus animals and trainers.

Go!
A referee with a megaphone can signal to each racer when to start. The referee can time each racer or the audience can clap, stomp, and cheer for their favorite circus-character racers. Won't the athletic acrobat be surprised when clumsy Ruffles the Clown qualifies for the final round! It could happen, so be prepared.

After circus performers have shown the audience how the course works, invite volunteers from the audience to demonstrate their nimbleness. Everyone will enjoy cheering on the racers!

joke
Knock, knock.
—Who's there?
Arthur.
—Arthur who?
Arthur more clowns in the circus?

Stilt Walking

Walking on stilts will make you look extra tall and show off your incredible balance. Master this skill and use it in your clown and acrobat acts.

Beginner Stilts

The audience will love watching you clomp across the circus ring on these simple stilts.

Materials
* 2 empty tomato cans that are the same large size, opened at one end
* length of rope (an old skipping rope works well)
* punch can opener
* scissors
* duct tape

1. Turn one can upside down and punch a hole on each side.
2. Repeat with the other can.
3. Have an adult tape over any sharp edges on the cans.
4. Hold one end of the rope and measure from your armpits to the ground. Double this length and cut the rope. Cut another piece the same length.
5. Thread the end of one piece of rope through one hole. Thread the other end of the piece of rope through the other hole.
6. Tie the two ends together inside the container. Make sure the knot is strong.
7. Repeat steps 5 and 6 to make the other stilt.

Voilà! Your stilts are done!

joke
Q: Forty people paid for admission to the circus. But the Ringmaster counted 44 heads. How is this possible?
A: He counted 40 foreheads.

Circus Lore

In the early days of Cirque du Soleil, stilt walking played a big role in raising enough money to make the circus possible. A very determined street performer named Gilles Ste-Croix from Quebec walked an astonishing 90 km (56 miles) on stilts to raise money for Cirque. This high-rise clomp between towns took him 22 hours and attracted lots of spectators and oodles of journalists from radio and TV. Cirque received their start-up funding, and the rest—as they say—is history.

Big Kid Stilts

If you are a big kid (over seven years old), you might like the challenge of using wooden stilts. Ask an adult to help you build these stilts.

Materials

- **one 2 x 2 piece of wood** (about 10 feet/3 m long)
- **one 2 x 4 piece of wood** (6 inches/15 cm long)
- **6 wood screws** (3 inch/7.6 cm)
- **measuring tape**
- **pencil**
- **handsaw**
- **drill**
- **screwdriver**
- **sandpaper**
- **plane** (optional, but nice!)

1. Cut the length of 2 x 2 in half to make two stilts. The stilts should be slightly longer than your height. (If you are 4 feet/120 cm tall, you'll want your stilts to be about 5 feet/150 cm tall.)
2. Cut the 2 x 4 in half to make two footrests. You can cut it on an angle to make streamlined footrests.
3. Sand the footrests.
4. Decide how high you want the footrests to be off the ground. Drill three holes (about 1 inch/2.5 cm apart) in each stilt at the chosen height. Make sure the two footrests are at the same height.
5. Screw the footrests to the stilts with the wood screws.
6. For more comfortable stilts, you can plane the corners on the upper half of your stilts and sand the edges of the footrests to smooth them.

Practice Tip
Have a friend or grown-up walk beside you as you practice. If you take a little tumble, your friend can catch you and soften the fall. Another tip is to take wee baby steps as you are learning. It's not a race!

Safety Smarts
Wear a bicycle or hockey helmet, knee pads, wrist protectors, and elbow pads. These will keep you safe if you fall. And make sure you practice in a large, flat, grassy area. Yup, it's smart to wear sneakers, too—not flip-flops!

Tightrope

Show your death-defying courage by walking a tightrope and reaching for the clouds. In your circus, you'll be able to do the impossible!

Faking the Setup #1

Walking the tightrope for real means going to circus school, training hard, and studying with the pros. But if running off to the circus is not in your future—at least not this week—don't despair. The backyard version is a cinch! Make up a circus act using a fake high wire. All you have to do is find a long skipping rope and stretch it out nice and straight on the ground. Then spread a beach towel neatly at each end of the rope. No wrinkles. The towels are not towels, you see, they are "resting platforms." They'll show the audience where the high wire ends. Use mime techniques when you pretend to climb way, way up an imaginary high ladder to the—yes, you've got it—resting platform.

Faking the Setup #2

A second way to fake a tightrope is to use a homemade balance beam. The balance beam should be extremely low to the ground. A balance beam is wider than a rope, but never fear—you can pretend it is narrow. The Ringmaster can help you out by telling the audience that you are about to walk across a tightrope that's high in the air. This will help to set up the act before you begin. Hold an umbrella in one hand and pretend it's helping you balance. Now, ham it up!

—Okay, now how's this all sounding to you?
—Pretty good. But do you really think the neighbors will believe that I'm on a high wire when the rope is sitting right there on the grass?
—Sure they will! If you believe it, they'll believe it. It's all about putting on a good show.
—But you don't have to worry about falling and cracking your head, right?
—Exactly! That's the real bonus of the fake high-wire act!

Now What?

Okay, now that you're "on the wire," let's see what neat tricks you can do. Use your gymnastic skills, dance moves, and clowning abilities to come up with a sizzling act. You'll want to use mime techniques to make the audience believe that you really are way up high in the sky. Show fear on your face with wide eyes and clenched teeth. Make yourself teeter to and fro on the wire as you try to do a move. A little suspense will help the audience to believe you're doing death-defying tricks, even when you are safely on the ground.

Pssst!
Tightrope walkers are called *funambulists*. How fun!

joke
Q: What's the hardest part about learning to ride a unicycle?
A: The ground.

Tightrope Stunts

If you want to come up with more high-wire stunts, think about the kinds of moves gymnasts do on the balance beam. All of these moves take place in a straight line, just like the tightrope. When you want to turn on the high wire, walk to the end and use the resting platform to turn around.

Cartwheels

The perfect cartwheel is one where your arms and legs all land in a straight line along the ground. Practice doing cartwheels in a straight line. Can you do this on top of the skipping-rope high wire?

Somersaults

It may be too tricky to do a somersault on a high wire, but if you're using a rope on the grass, it is totally possible. The ground will support you. The cool thing is that you can make the audience believe you are rolling on a thin wire suspended in the air. Now that's impressive!

Arabesques

How about some ballet positions? An arabesque is a pose that would look lovely on the high wire. Stand on one tiptoe (in ballet talk this is called demi-pointe) and stretch the other leg out behind you. Keep your toe pointed and your leg straight. If you are very flexible, you can try to raise your leg up to the height of your waist. Gracefully raise one arm above your head and stretch the other arm behind you. Hold your fingers in a soft, elegant position. Often, in an arabesque, your arms mirror your legs. That is, if you are stretching the left arm behind you, the left leg should also be stretched out beautifully behind your body.

Leaps and Jumps

The tightrope is a great place to try jumps and leaps. Experiment to find your personal faves. You can do a snappy scissors jump along the length of the wire. A tight tuck jump looks great in the middle of the wire. To finish a routine, you could try a star jump from the end of the wire onto the platform. At the end of each jump, bend your knees and use your arms to help to find your balance again.

Balancing Tricks

High-wire acts often show performers balancing things. Place a hardcover book on your head. Let go with your hands, hold your head high, and walk across the wire. Another idea is to collect giant stuffed animals and balance one or two on your back as you cross the wire. Pretend they are oh so very heavy by hunching over and showing the effort on your face.

Wheelbarrow Race

Okay, it's not really a race here, but you know the wheelbarrow race position, right? Find a partner and decide who will be the wheelbarrow and who will be the one pushing the wheelbarrow. Both performers must place their hands or feet directly on the tightrope line as they cross it. (This is harder than the usual wheelbarrow race, where the wheelbarrow person can place her hands shoulder-width apart.) *Wo-ooa-oah!* Try not to tip over!

> A clown went to the doctor and said, "Doctor, I cut my ear!"
> The doctor said, "How'd you do that, Max?"
> The clown replied, "I bit it."
> "You can't bite your own ear!" said the doctor.
> The clown replied, "Oh, but I stood on a chair!"

Novelty Acts

Magic Show

Magicians can mystify the crowd with spellbinding tricks! How about making a scarf suddenly appear, a pencil stick to your hand, and a penny vanish?

Costume Materials

You can dress like a conventional magician with a top hat and bow tie. Or you could present yourself as a crafty wizard with a cone-shaped hat and long cape. A clown dressed in a typical clown suit can do magic tricks, too. Look around for costume materials like these:

* top hat
* wizard hat
* bow tie
* cape
* wand
* scarves

Equipment

A stool or chair could be useful for your act. A star-and-moon tablecloth is great if you have one, but any old tablecloth or sheet will do. Some dollar stores sell plain paper tablecloths, which are fun because you can decorate them yourself. You'll need a place to store your props that keeps them hidden from the audience. Do you have an old suitcase? Cool! Decorate the front of the suitcase with stick-on stars and a moon, or magic dust made from glitter glue. You could also decorate a cardboard box to store your supplies in. Wow! You're looking so professional!

Props

Magicians always have a large collection of props, from trick cards to whoopee cushions. Here are some of the basic props that can fill your box of tricks:

* deck of cards
* rope
* table tennis balls
* coins
* stuffed rabbit
* rubber snakes and spiders

If you want to add music to your magic act, choose something lively and strong to create the best atmosphere. These classical pieces are very dramatic and work well for magic shows:

* Georges Bizet's "Les Toréadors" from *Carmen Suite*
* Johann Strauss Jr.'s "Tritch Tratch Polka"
* J.P. Sousa's "Liberty Bell"
* Ludwig van Beethoven's Fifth Symphony

If none of the parents have these recordings, try the public library or online music collections.

Simple Tricks

There are lots of fun, simple magic tricks. To fool your audience, be sure to practice the tricks you will perform over and over. The more you practice, the faster your hands will move. Practice will also make the performance talk, or "patter," sound more polished. A good magician must be confident in his talent and in the way he sounds. It's all about being *smooooooth*.

Sneaky Scarf Trick

Wear a cardigan or jacket. Feed one end of a very long scarf up through one sleeve. Then thread the scarf across your back and down the other sleeve. Tug on one end of the scarf so that it is just barely peeking out from your sleeve at your wrist. Make sure the scarf is on the inside of your arm so that the end is hidden.

Once you're in front of the audience, start by saying magical nonsense phrases such as **"Hocus Pocus, Kalamazoo, Rinkitty, Pinkitty, Zip Plip Flew!"** Wave your arms around mysteriously. Tell the crowd that you are going to perform a sneaky scarf trick. Quickly, in one sharp movement, tug the end of the scarf (*whoosh!*) so that the entire length of scarf appears in a long, twisty ribbon of color.

Magician Patter

Patter is what magicians say to the audience as they perform. Often they seem to talk non-stop. Patter is used to distract the audience from seeing what the magician is hiding. Patter can make the audience focus on the left hand while the right hand is busy hiding the "disappearing" object.

Magic Pencil

Find a wooden pencil and roll up your sleeves. Tell the audience that you are going to make the pencil magically stick to your palm. Show the pencil to an audience member and ask this person to examine it. Ask, "Is it sticky?" Once everyone knows it is just an ordinary pencil, you can start the tricky stuff.

1. Place the pencil on your palm, holding the pencil with your thumb.
2. Hold this same arm straight up with your palm away from the audience.
3. Grasp your wrist so that three fingers and your thumb face the audience.
4. Position your pointer finger straight up the palm of your hand, holding the pencil in place.
5. Say: "Now watch as I remove my thumb." Extend your thumb. It will look as if the pencil is stuck to your hand. The audience won't realize that one of the fingers grasping your wrist is missing! Then move the pencil up and down your palm with your pointer finger. Exclaim: "Presto! The pencil is floating!"

Practice this trick until you can do all the steps quickly.

Give 'Em an Earful!
Go for some laughs by tucking the pencil behind your ear and pretending you've lost it. Look high and low before you finally listen to the audience yelling, "It's behind your ear!" Grab the pencil and laugh sheepishly before getting back to the Magic Pencil trick.

Experienced magicians can do more difficult tricks like the "classic palm." By gently squeezing the muscles in the palm of their hand, they can hide a small object, like a coin, in the center.

joke
Q: What do you call a lion with a toothache?
A: Rory!

The Vanishing Penny

All you need for this trick is a penny. Tuck in your shirt and follow these steps:

1. Show the audience the penny and ask, "Does this look magical?" Then place the penny in the palm of one hand.
2. With the penny cupped in your palm, begin to rub the penny against your opposite elbow. Announce: "I am going to rub this penny and make it disappear!"
3. Make the penny seem to accidentally fall from your hand onto the ground. "Whoops!"
4. Lean over to pick up the penny with the hand you were rubbing with. As you straighten up, lifting the penny, quickly drop it into the "elbow hand." This switch requires lots of practice, but once you've got the hang of it, the audience will be fooled. They'll think the penny is still in the hand you are rubbing with, because the hand is faster than the eye!
5. Drop the penny down the back of your shirt.
6. Rub your elbow with great gusto. Look at your elbow as you rub it.
7. Smile as you lift your palm a little from your elbow. Whisper loudly to the audience, "I think it's nearly gone!"
8. Wiggle your fingers theatrically as you remove your empty palm from your elbow. Announce proudly: "Ta-da! The penny has disappeared!" Grin triumphantly and show your empty hand to the audience. Take a bow.

joke
Q: What steps should you take if a lion is chasing you?
A: Long, quick ones.

Talk to the Mirror

Stand in front of a mirror when you practice your magic tricks. Make big gestures with your hands. Watch in the mirror to make sure you are hiding the "disappearing" objects successfully. Use your voice to build up the suspense of each trick. Your face can show excitement, concentration, worry, surprise, and delight as you perform.

Mime

Mime is a silent style of acting. Mime artists create objects and settings by moving their hands and body in special ways. When clowns perform mime, a sudden hush can fall over the normally noisy circus tent. Mime can be truly mesmerizing!

Costume Suggestions

Sometimes mime artists dress like clowns, if the act suits it, but simple black costumes are ideal for performing mime.

- black pants or tights
- black T-shirt or tank top
- bodysuit
- black bowler hat
- plain vest
- black ballet slippers or bare feet

Create an Illusion

Like magic, mime centers around the wonderful world of illusions. The mime artist uses his gestures, movements, and clear facial expressions to make the audience believe something is there even when it isn't. By carefully feeling the imaginary surface of a wall, the mime artist can make the audience believe that there is a massive brick wall on stage. Or a mime artist can pretend to blow up a balloon, lick an ice-cream cone, play tennis, or do any other normal activity. The "props" (balloon, ice-cream cone, tennis rackets, and ball) are invisible, but the audience is willing to pretend they are there.

When you practice mime, you'll want to perfect the big arm gestures and silly facial expressions you use. If you become distracted during a performance and laugh or make a sloppy move, the audience may snap out of their "I-believe-you" state of mind. Your job is to make sure that your actions and gestures look real. Practice is the key!

Mime Tips
- Make clear and exaggerated gestures. Keep those movements big!
- Using your face and body, show strong emotions: happiness, sadness, surprise, fear, and anger.
- Focus really well and try not to speak or giggle.

Modern Mime

Marcel Marceau is a master of modern-day mime. He is a French artist who created his own form of silent mime. He looked up to Charlie Chaplin, a silent screen actor from the early days of black-and-white film. Marcel Marceau says it all without actually saying anything! In 1947, Marceau invented the character of a white-faced clown named Bip. Most people, when they think of mime, picture the amazing Marcel Marceau.

The Roots of Mime

Unlike modern-day mime artists, who are silent, historical mime artists spoke. Mime was around way back in ancient Greece. At the famous Theater of Dionysus in Athens, actors used really big gestures. Later, in the early 1500s, actors often wearing masks performed skits in the streets of Italy. This mime was known as *commedia dell'arte* (comedy of the artists). The actors played well-known characters like Arlecchio (Harlequin), a poor man who outwits the rich, and Pedrolino, a sad white-faced clown. They made up or improvised dialogue. Their large gestures and expressive faces helped the audience understand them no matter what language people spoke.

Funny Skits

Short mime skits are perfect in between more complicated circus acts. To get started, just focus on a simple everyday event, then think of all the funny things that could happen.

1. Brush your teeth, swishing water in your puffed-out cheeks.
2. Put on lipstick, peering into a mirror with kissy lips.
3. Peel and eat a banana, then slip on the peel.

You can also try out other circus acts, such as juggling and weightlifting—they'll be way easier to do with mime. Then, for more of a challenge, try miming these funny situations:

1. Walk into wet cement on a new sidewalk.
2. Paint yourself into a corner.
3. Eat cotton candy on a bus, lurching from side to side.

Use your imagination to think up lots of other hilarious events!

joke
Q: Why did the clown wear loud socks?
A: So his feet wouldn't fall asleep.

Strongman

Find the "World's Strongest Man" or the "World's Strongest Woman" by hosting a weightlifting contest under the big top!

Make the audience believe that you are the strongest weightlifter in the world by making fake barbells that are light as a feather—well, almost!

Faking It #1

Make lightweight barbells with a cardboard tube from a roll of wrapping paper and four aluminum pie plates. Ask an adult to help you cut an "X" slit in the center of each pie plate. Tape two pie plates together, facing, to form a disc shape. Wiggle the disc onto one end of the tube. Fit the other two pie plates onto the other end. Use a little more tape to secure the pie-plate weights to the bar.

> Strong women doing amazing feats of strength and stamina are celebrated in many modern circuses, such as Circus Oz. Whether they are catching a partner on the trapeze or spinning inside a giant wheel, these women have MUSCLE!!!

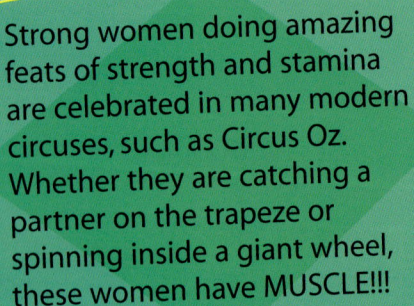

Deadlift Technique

Begin by having a whole team of participants haul out the barbell, perhaps on a wagon. This will show that it is incredibly heavy.

Stand behind the bar with your feet shoulder-width apart. Grasp the bar, look up, and take a big gulp of air. Pull the barbell off the ground as you straighten your knees and back. (Don't forget to show the huge strain in your face!) Grin as the bar reaches thigh level. Wait for applause, then slowly lower the bar back down to the ground, bending your knees and back. Collapse onto the ground, exhausted.

Faking It #2

Another (messier!) method is to make ball-shaped weights for the ends of the cardboard tube. You can make balls using papier-mâché.

—What's all this faking it about? Why can't I just do some real powerlifting?
—No way! Save the real thing for the gym. You'll entertain your audience much more with a power-lifting act that looks so incredible, it defies gravity and about 14 other natural laws.
—But won't they know it's fake?
—Na. They'll be so caught up in watching you act like it's real that they'll start to believe it *is* real. Besides, faking it is way safer. If you do real weightlifting, you'll need a couple of "spotters" and the act will just become too darned serious.
—And "entertainment" is the name of the game?
—Precisely, my friend! So ham it up and have some fun.
—All right. I get it now.

Materials
* **cardboard tube from a roll of wrapping paper**
* **2 medium-sized balloons**
* **flour**
* **water**
* **newspaper**
* **bowl**
* **scissors**
* **tape**
* **black paint**

1. Blow up two balloons to about the same size.
2. Place a cup (250 ml) of flour, a teaspoon (5 ml) of salt, and two cups (500 ml) of water in a bowl and mix well.
3. Cut up strips of newspaper into 3 cm x 20 cm (1" x 8") lengths.
4. Dip a strip of paper into the runny paste and then plaster the paper onto the outside of the balloon.
5. Keep layering the strips of paper onto the balloon until the whole surface is covered. Make sure the lengths overlap and cross each other in different directions. Leave a small spot around the balloon's knot uncovered. This is where the tube will fit into the ball.
6. Repeat with the other balloon and let the papier-mâché dry for a few days.
7. If there are gaps in the papier-mâché, you can mix up more paste and add another layer.
8. Use scissors to make bigger holes so that the balls will fit onto each end of the cardboard tube. Tape the balls in place and paint the barbells black.

Come One, Come All!

The performance date is two weeks away! It's time to make sure the whole neighborhood knows about the show.

Posters

Exciting, colorful posters will attract the attention of friends and neighbors who might not know about the show. If there is a bulletin board in your community, ask if you can hang a poster there. You might also ask your school, recreation center, or local store if they will let you put up a poster. The name of the game is to get the word out.

Materials
* heavy paper or bristol board
* pencil
* markers
* crayons
* stickers, glitter, glue, ribbons, and balloons (optional)

Start off by writing the information on your piece of paper in pencil. This way, you can experiment with the size and position of letters on the poster. There's nothing worse than writing out a long word like "fabulous" and running out of space halfway through the word! Be sure to include:

* the name of the circus
* the date
* the time
* the place
* the price, if you will charge admission

Include a few exciting headings in big letters that advertise your major acts, such as:

Clowns! Jugglers! Stilt Walking! Magicians! and more!

Check over all the information (and your spelling), then trace over the words with brilliant colors. Dress up the poster by adding a drawing of a clown, a circus tent, or a juggler. When people spot a cheerful picture of a circusy character, they'll immediately know the poster is for a circus or a fun family event. Then they'll run over to read the details. Next thing you know, they'll be telling their friends, and so on until EVERYONE knows! Hey, it's also a good idea to make some extra posters to decorate the ticket-taking area on the day of the circus.

Invitations

If you want to give out special invitations to anyone—family, friends, neighbors—use the same materials listed for poster making, but make cards instead of posters. You can fold the paper into cards or make postcard-style invitations.

Tickets

Decide if you will sell (or give away) tickets in advance. If you decide to sell tickets, you could use the profits to buy materials for your next show, treat the performers to something yummy, or donate the money to charity.

If you do sell tickets ahead of time, include the time and place on the tickets, so people remember. Number the tickets so that you can keep track of how many are sold. You might give each performer five tickets to sell or give away a few days before the show.

Thank-You List

On the days leading up to the show, make a list of all the people who helped. Think about who helped you find costumes and props, who loaned you equipment, and who helped make things. Pass the list around to all the performers to make sure no one is overlooked. Parents and friends will appreciate being thanked for their assistance. Also, if they know how much you appreciate them, they'll be more willing to help again next time!

Neat and Tidy

Make your invitations and posters really exciting, but also neat and tidy. This is important because these advertisements are the first circus-related things people will see. Make a good first impression. This tells your family, friends, and neighbors that you've worked hard on the show and that it will be polished and entertaining.

Big Top Time!

Final Go-Through!

A couple of days before the show, you might want to practice all the acts in order with costumes and props. This will help to make everything go smoothly on the big day.

Spiffing Up

Urge the performers to arrive an hour before the show. Have a couple of kids set up chairs for the audience. Choose one or two others to deck out the entrance area. You'll want to stick up those snazzy extra posters and set up the ticket booth.

Goof-Proof Booths

A simple ticket-taking area could be a container for money and a container for tickets, sitting on a chair. Decorate the chair with a cheerful bouquet of balloons.

A fancier style of ticket booth could be a decorated card table or patio table. Or you can use a really big cardboard box. Cut a square hole in the box to make a window for the ticket takers. Decorate your booth with colorful paints, streamers, and, of course, balloons.

Behind-the-Scenes Setup

Go over the checklists for props, costumes, and equipment to be sure you have everything. Next, have each performer put their costumes and props in a box with their name on it—this makes them easier to find. Make sure the Stage Manager and the Ringmaster have a clear list of the acts in the right order. Post a copy of this list in the behind-the-scenes area so that performers can see which act is up next. After that, set up a face-painting station with a table and chairs and a few mirrors. Then cheer and do a little dance—it's all really happening! *Yeah!!!* Apply the clown makeup. Put on your costumes. Make sure all the players are ready for the first act. Finally, check the stereo and make sure your music is arranged neatly in a box.

Pssst!

The area around the main entrance to the circus, where tickets and refreshments are sold, is called the *midway*.

Step Right Up!

Shout It Out!
You want to attract as big a crowd as possible, so, about 20 minutes before the circus begins, you may want to start shouting to people on the street! Have your ticket takers, ushers, and any performers who are ready yell out popular circus phrases from page 6, such as "Come One, Come All!" and "Step Right Up, Folks." You can also highlight a few of the acts and say something like "See Acrobatic Abby perform an amazing balancing trick!"

Go With the Flow
Don't worry if the acts don't go exactly as planned. Be ready to improvise and go with the flow. If someone forgets to say or do something, it could make the act even funnier than you planned! Unexpected changes and surprises during rehearsed acts can jack up the fun factor, because the performers will have to react quickly. Improvising keeps everyone on their toes.

In a Muddle? Pandemonium Fix-It
If everyone forgets their lines, a prop falls apart, or a performer catches a bad case of the giggles, don't worry, there is a solution. Call on the Ringmaster to end that particular act immediately. *Whew!* Then have the Ringmaster tell a few jokes and introduce the next act. Later, you can present the unfinished act again, avoiding the things that made it go off course the first time. After all, you've spent a lot of time on this—you don't want to cancel an act completely. With any luck, the second attempt will go much more smoothly.

> When things get crazy and you have to stop an act, you can always "bring on the clowns" to keep the audience chuckling.

joke
Q: What kind of bow can't be tied?
A: A rainbow.

After the Show

At the end of the show, have everyone take a bow and soak up that wonderful applause. Doesn't it feel great? All that hard work paid off!

What's Next?

How do you feel now that it's all over? Tired? Happy? Relieved? A little sad? Or are you already thinking up ideas for the next show? If so, grab your notebook and jot them down now. Don't delay or you might forget some stupendous acts! You can stow them away safely in a shoe box for next time. Throughout the year, whenever you think of something new, write it down and toss the paper into the box. Winter is a great time for brainstorming ideas and starting to write. It's fun to make the backyard circus a yearly summer event, so try to keep the tradition going—and keep an eye out for new recruits!

Have fun with your next backyard circus!

Thank you! Thank you!

All the performers should give a big thank you to the family who hosted the backyard circus show. If you took turns practicing in many neighbors' backyards, you should thank all those people. One idea is to have the Ringmaster announce all the people who helped out with the show after you take your bows. Another wonderful way to say thanks is to make thank-you cards for all the helpers.

Scrub, Wipe, and Polish

Once everyone has had some time to talk about the show and bask in the glory, gather the participants together again for the cleanup. Make sure everyone collects his or her own costume pieces and props. Wipe up any spills and pick up any garbage, including broken bits of balloons.

Circus Lore

Many modern circuses hold auditions in cities around the world and hire talent scouts. The scouts visit circus schools, sports clubs, and cultural events to check out kids and adults who have special abilities. Imagine doing backflips and tumbling moves at a gymnastics club when suddenly a circus scout decides you have what it takes! It's true that some lucky kids do get discovered this way, but if you want to join a circus troupe someday, you'll have to practice lots. Think big and see where your dreams take you!

Fun Resources for Further Exploration

Cassidy, John, and the Editors of *Klutz*. *The Klutz Yo-Yo Book*. Palo Alto, CA: Klutz, 1998.

Dunleavy, Deborah; Jane Kurisu, illus. *The Jumbo Book of Drama*. Toronto, ON: Kids Can Press, 2004.

Friedman, Lise; photographs by Mary Dowdle. *Break a Leg!: The Kids' Guide to Acting and Stagecraft*. New York, NY: Workman Publishing, 2002.

Granfield, Linda. *Circus*. Toronto, ON: Groundwood, 1997.

Irving, Robert, and Mike Martins. *Pathways in Juggling. Learn How to Juggle with Balls, Clubs, Devil Sticks, Diabolos, and Beyond*. Toronto, ON: Firefly Books, 1997.

Jackman, Joan. *The Young Gymnast: A Young Enthusiast's Guide to Gymnastics*. New York, NY: Dorling Kindersley, 1995.

Jaffe, Elizabeth Dana. *Juggling*. (Games Around the World series.) Minneapolis, MN: Compass Point Books, 2002.

Klingel, Cynthia, and Robert B. Noyed. *Yo-Yo Tricks*. (Games Around the World series.) Minneapolis, MN: Compass Point Books, 2002.

Marceau, Marcel, and Bruce Goldstone; photographs by Steven Rothfeld. *Bip in a Book*. New York, NY: Stewart, Tabori & Chang, 2001.

Silver, Patricia. *Face Painting*. (Kids Can Do It series.) Toronto, ON: Kids Can Press, 2000.

Websites

The addresses of websites can change often. If you have trouble finding a site, try using a search engine or check with a librarian for current listings.

Big Apple Circus	www.bigapplecircus.org
Cirque du Soleil	www.cirquedusoleil.com
Cirque Éloize	www.cirque-eloize.com
Circus Ethiopia	www.lefourneau.com/artistes/circus
Circus Oz	www.circusoz.com
Circus! Trivia	www.ontariosciencecentre.ca/media/default.asp?releaseid=549
How to Devil Stick	www.yoyoguy.com/info/devilstick/
The Instant Jugglers' Manual	www.yoyoguy.com/info/ball/index2.html
The Science of Juggling	www2.bc.edu/~lewbel/jugweb/science-1.html
Ringling Bros. and Barnum & Bailey	www.ringling.com

Circus Schools

Circus schools hold summer camps and weekend classes. These schools are excellent resource centers for backyard circus performers. You can also check them out on the Web.

Atlantic Cirque Agency & School
Dartmouth, Nova Scotia, CANADA

École Nationale de Cirque/National Circus School
Montréal, Quebec, CANADA

Toronto School of Circus Arts
Toronto, Ontario, CANADA

The CirKids School of Circus Arts
Vancouver, British Columbia, CANADA

Circus Juventas
St. Paul, Minnesota, USA

Summer Smirkus Camp
Craftsbury Common, Vermont, USA

The Circus Space
London, UK

Blackpool Circus School
Blackpool, Lancashire, UK

About the Author
Jill Bryant had a fabulous childhood in Elora, Ontario, that was filled with make-believe games, adventures in forts, and, of course, backyard circuses. Gymnastics, pogo sticking, and unicycling were among her favorite childhood activities. While earning an Honors Bachelor of Arts degree from the University of Waterloo, Jill became keenly interested in children's books. Jill is the author of *Amazing Women Athletes*, and the co-author of *Making Shadow Puppets*. Since 2000, Jill has lived in Halifax, Nova Scotia; Princeton, New Jersey; and Manchester, England. She lives with her husband and their two daughters.

About the Illustrator
Stephen MacEachern is an accomplished graphic designer and the illustrator of many books, including *38 Ways to Entertain Your Babysitter*, *The Kids Guide to Money Cents*, and *Switched On, Flushed Down, Tossed Out: Investigating the Hidden Workings of Your Home*.

Acknowledgements
Special thanks to my husband, Daryn Lehoux; my mom, Bonnie McTaggart; my dad, Gary Bryant; and also Carolyn Miller, Carol McDougall, Sharon E. McKay, Katharina Zinn, and Susan Hanna MacQueen. Thank you to Woozles, Frog Hollow Books, and the Writers' Federation of Nova Scotia. Warm thanks to editor Pamela Robertson. —J.B.